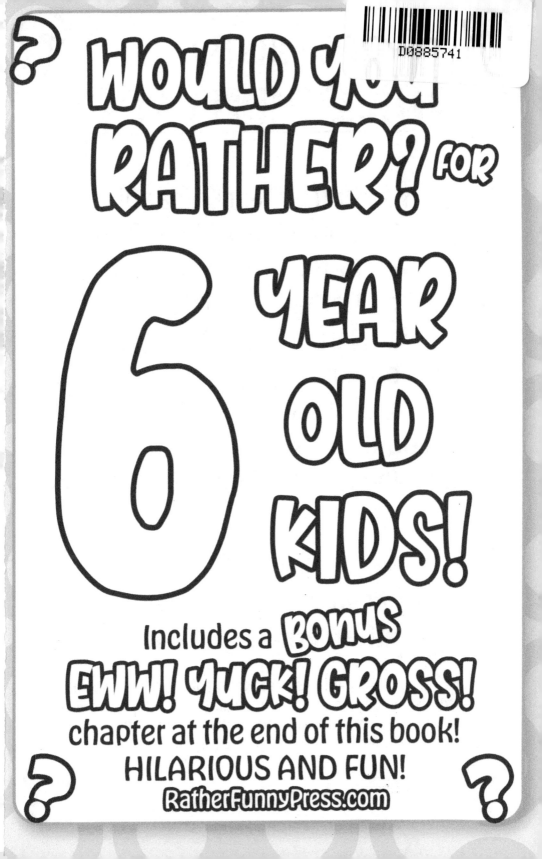

WOULD YOU RATHER? FOR

6 YEAR OLD KIDS!

Includes a BONUS
EWW! YUCK! GROSS!
chapter at the end of this book!
HILARIOUS AND FUN!
RatherFunnyPress.com

Books By
RATHER FUNNY PRESS

Would You Rather? For 6 Year Old Kids!
Would You Rather? For 7 Year Old Kids!
Would You Rather? For 8 Year Old Kids!
Would You Rather? For 9 Year Old Kids!
Would You Rather? For 10 Year Old Kids!
Would You Rather? For 11 Year Old Kids!
Would You Rather? For 12 Year Old Kids!
Would You Rather? For Teens!
Would You Rather? Eww! Yuck! Gross!

To see all the latest books by
Rather Funny Press just go to
RatherFunnyPress.com

YOUR FREE SURPRISE GIFT!

Details on the last page of this book!
A brand new free joke book
just for you.
Check it out! Laughter awaits!

RatherFunnyPress.com

HOW TO PLAY

This easy to play game is a ton of fun!
Have 2 or more players.
The first reader will choose a 'Would You Rather?'
from the book and read it aloud.
The other player(s) then choose which scenario
they would prefer and why.
You can't say 'neither' or 'none'.
You must choose one and explain why.
Then the book is passed to the next person
and the game continues!

The main rule is have fun, laugh and enjoy
spending time with your friends and family.
Let the fun begin!

ATTENTION!

All the scenarios and choices in this book are
fictional and meant to be about using your
imagination, having a ton of fun and enjoying this
game with your friends and family.
Obviously, DO NOT ATTEMPT any of these
scenarios in real life.

RatherFunnyPress.com

WOULD YOU RATHER...

WAKE UP WITH ANGEL'S WINGS

OR

A DOG'S TAIL?

BE UNABLE TO CONTROL HOW FAST YOU TALK

OR

HOW LOUD YOU TALK?

WOULD YOU RATHER...

ROLL DOWN A MILE LONG HILL

OR

DIVE 20 FEET INTO A POOL?

HAVE RABBIT EARS

OR

A PIG NOSE?

WOULD YOU RATHER...

SWIM IN A POOL OF YOUR FAVORITE SODA

OR

SWIM IN A POOL OF MILK?

MAKE THE WORLD'S BIGGEST PIZZA

OR

THE WORLD'S BIGGEST PANCAKE?

WOULD YOU RATHER...

LIVE IN A HOUSE MADE OF VEGETABLES

OR

A HOUSE MADE OF MEAT?

HAVE A PET DRAGON

OR

A PET UNICORN?

WOULD YOU RATHER...

HAVE A HOME COOKED MEAL

OR

FAST FOOD?

MEET A PUPPY THAT WALKS ON TWO LEGS

OR

A PUPPY THAT TALKS?

WOULD YOU RATHER...

GET STUNG BY A BEE

OR

SCRATCHED BY A CAT?

LIVE ON THE SPACE STATION

OR

IN A CASTLE?

WOULD YOU RATHER...

BE A MERMAID

OR

A UNICORN?

SEE A SHOOTING STAR

OR

A BEAUTIFUL RAINBOW?

WOULD YOU RATHER...

HAVE A PET WORM

OR

A PET SNAIL?

BE A GHOST

OR

A VAMPIRE?

WOULD YOU RATHER...

NOT BE ABLE TO HEAR

OR

NOT BE ABLE TO SEE?

SPEND EVERY WINTER
AT THE SNOW

OR

EVERY SUMMER AT
THE BEACH?

WOULD YOU RATHER...

HAVE A BOY

OR

A GIRL AS
YOUR BEST FRIEND?

NEVER CUT YOUR HAIR AGAIN

OR

NEVER SHOWER AGAIN?

WOULD YOU RATHER...

BE A TRAIN DRIVER

OR

A BUS DRIVER?

EAT A WHOLE RAW ONION

OR

A WHOLE LEMON?

WOULD YOU RATHER...

HAVE A PET DRAGON

OR

A PET DINOSAUR?

DANCE FOR 3 HOURS A DAY

OR

SING FOR 3 HOURS A DAY?

WOULD YOU RATHER...

CHANGE THE COLOR OF
YOUR HAIR

OR

YOUR EYES?

WASH YOUR HAIR WITH
ORANGE JUICE

OR

BRUSH YOUR TEETH WITH
KETCHUP?

WOULD YOU RATHER...

BE BAREFOOT FOR THE REST OF YOUR LIFE

OR

WEAR HIGH HEELS FOR THE REST OF YOUR LIFE?

WEAR A CLOWN NOSE

OR

CLOWN SHOES?

WOULD YOU RATHER...

LIVE ON A VERY HIGH MOUNTAIN

OR

A TROPICAL ISLAND?

BE A SUPERHERO

OR

A MAGICAL WIZARD?

WOULD YOU RATHER...

HAVE REALLY LONG LEGS

OR

REALLY SHORT LEGS?

HAVE A SNOWBALL FIGHT

OR

A WATER BALLOON FIGHT?

WOULD YOU RATHER...

HAVE PURPLE HAIR

OR

ORANGE EYES?

RIDE A GIANT KITTEN

OR

A BIG PUPPY?

WOULD YOU RATHER...

BE AN ASTRONAUT

OR

A RACE CAR DRIVER?

STEP ON A LEGO

OR

STEP IN DOG POO?

WOULD YOU RATHER...

BE SUPERMAN

OR

SUPERGIRL?

WALK BAREFOOT FOR A MILE IN HOT SAND

OR

FREEZING COLD SNOW?

WOULD YOU RATHER...

NEVER BRUSH YOUR
TEETH AGAIN

OR

NEVER WASH YOUR
HAIR AGAIN?

WEAR PINK CLOTHES

OR

BLUE CLOTHES?

WOULD YOU RATHER...

NEVER EAT CANDY AGAIN

OR

NEVER WATCH TV AGAIN?

CLIMB A TREE

OR

GO DOWN A WATER SLIDE?

WOULD YOU RATHER...

HAVE A SIDE DISH OF BROCCOLI

OR

FRENCH FRIES?

LIVE AT AN AMUSEMENT PARK

OR

A BOWLING ALLEY?

WOULD YOU RATHER...

SHOWER WITH ONLY
COLD WATER

OR

ONLY HOT WATER?

GET TO SCHOOL BY RIDING
A HORSE

OR

BY BOUNCING ALL THE WAY ON
A POGO STICK?

WOULD YOU RATHER...

GO TO BED VERY LATE
EVERY NIGHT

OR

GET UP REALLY EARLY
EVERY MORNING?

HAVE A PET KANGAROO THAT
CAN SPEAK ENGLISH

OR

A PET CAT THAT IS BIG
ENOUGH TO RIDE?

WOULD YOU RATHER...

RUN REALLY FAST

OR

JUMP REALLY HIGH?

PLAY HIDE AND SEEK

OR

PLAY CATCH?

WOULD YOU RATHER...

BE A KID FOR THE REST
OF YOUR LIFE

OR

BE A GROWN UP NOW?

EAT ONLY WITH A SPOON

OR

ONLY WITH A FORK?

WOULD YOU RATHER...

BE ALLERGIC TO PIZZA

OR

ALLERGIC TO CHOCOLATE?

GET CHASED BY 4 TURKEYS

OR

8 DUCKS?

WOULD YOU RATHER...

BE COVERED IN FUR

OR

COVERED IN FISH SCALES?

WEAR FISH SMELLING CLOTHES

OR

CLOTHES FIVE SIZES TOO BIG?

WOULD YOU RATHER...

EAT SNAIL FLAVORED
ICE CREAM

OR

DRINK ROTTEN EGG
FLAVORED SODA?

HAVE A FLUFFY CAT

OR

A FURRY DOG?

WOULD YOU RATHER...

BE A GOOD DANCER

OR

GOOD AT DRAWING?

HAVE A MAGIC FLYING CARPET

OR

A PET KANGAROO?

WOULD YOU RATHER...

RIDE A VERY BIG HORSE

OR

A VERY SMALL PONY?

HAVE ONE REALLY BIG EYE

OR

ONE REALLY BIG EAR?

WOULD YOU RATHER...

FLY A KITE

OR

SWING ON A SWING?

BE A RABBIT

OR

A TURTLE?

WOULD YOU RATHER...

EAT 6 HAMBURGERS

OR

6 HOT DOGS?

EAT A SPOONFUL
OF SUGAR

OR

A SPOONFUL OF SALT?

WOULD YOU RATHER...

SMILE WHEN YOU'RE SAD

OR

FROWN WHEN YOU'RE HAPPY?

BE ABLE TO ONLY HEAR VERY QUIET SOUNDS

OR

VERY LOUD SOUNDS?

WOULD YOU RATHER...

HOLD A GIANT SPIDER

OR

A GIANT COCKROACH?

HAVE THE HEAD OF A SHEEP

OR

THE BODY OF A SHEEP?

WOULD YOU RATHER...

CATCH ONE BIG FISH

OR

LOTS OF LITTLE FISH?

BE A BASKETBALL STAR

OR

A BASEBALL STAR?

WOULD YOU RATHER...

HAVE A ROBOT AS YOUR SERVANT

OR

BE A ROBOT?

HOP ALL THE WAY TO SCHOOL

OR

SKIP ALL THE WAY TO SCHOOL?

WOULD YOU RATHER...

BE ABLE TO READ THE
MINDS OF ANIMALS

OR

HUMANS?

HAVE 2 HANDS AT THE END
OF EACH ARM

OR

2 FEET AT THE END OF
EACH LEG?

WOULD YOU RATHER...

EAT LOTS OF CANDY

OR

LOTS OF FRUIT?

MAKE A HOUSE OUT OF PANCAKES

OR

A FORT OUT OF POPCORN?

WOULD YOU RATHER...

BE AN AMAZING DANCER

OR

A REALLY FAST RUNNER?

SLEEP FOR 5 HOURS
EVERY NIGHT

OR

10 HOURS EVERY
NIGHT?

WOULD YOU RATHER...

HANG OUT WITH ELSA FOR A DAY

OR

SHREK FOR A DAY?

WORK ON A FISHING BOAT

OR

IN A MUSEUM?

WOULD YOU RATHER...

HAVE ONE REALLY
LONG LEG

OR

ONE REALLY LONG ARM?

BRUSH YOUR TEETH
WITH MILK

OR

ORANGE JUICE?

WOULD YOU RATHER...

BE FRIENDS WITH
MICKEY MOUSE

OR

DORA THE EXPLORER?

HANG OUT WITH YOUR
FAMILY

OR

YOUR FRIENDS?

WOULD YOU RATHER...

BE GOOD AT SPORT

OR

GOOD WITH COMPUTERS?

GO SNOW SKIING

OR

GO TO A WATER PARK?

WOULD YOU RATHER...

BE A FIREMAN

OR

DRIVE AN AMBULANCE?

HAVE BRIGHT BLUE HAIR

OR

BRIGHT GREEN HAIR?

WOULD YOU RATHER...

CHANGE YOUR FIRST NAME

OR

YOUR MIDDLE NAME?

HAVE FINGERS ON YOUR FEET

OR

TOES ON YOUR HANDS?

WOULD YOU RATHER...

BE THIRSTY ALL THE TIME

OR

HUNGRY ALL THE TIME?

HAVE 3 PET ALLIGATORS

OR

3 PET TURTLES?

WOULD YOU RATHER...

BRUSH YOUR TEETH
WITH SOAP

OR

DRINK SOUR MILK?

HAVE A CUDDLE WITH
A LLAMA

OR

A KOALA BEAR?

WOULD YOU RATHER...

EAT A ROTTEN BANANA

OR

EAT A CUP FULL OF GRASS?

PLAY BASEBALL AS
THE PITCHER

OR

THE CATCHER?

WOULD YOU RATHER...

EAT 4 HOTDOGS

OR

A BIG PIZZA?

HAVE RABBIT EARS

OR

A MONKEY'S TAIL?

WOULD YOU RATHER...

HAVE ONLY 2 FINGERS ON EACH HAND

OR

ONLY 2 TOES ON EACH FOOT?

BE A TEACHER

OR

A DOCTOR?

WOULD YOU RATHER...

DRIVE A COOL RACE CAR

OR

FLY A HELICOPTER?

LIVE BY THE BEACH

OR

LIVE IN THE FOREST?

WOULD YOU RATHER...

HAVE CORN FOR TEETH

OR

SPAGHETTI FOR HAIR?

HAVE AN EXTRA EYE ON YOUR FOREHEAD

OR

AN EXTRA EYE ON THE BACK OF YOUR HEAD?

WOULD YOU RATHER...

HAVE REALLY COLD WEATHER

OR

REALLY HOT WEATHER?

RIDE A DONKEY TO SCHOOL

OR

A GIRAFFE TO SCHOOL?

WOULD YOU RATHER...

HAVE A PET WOODPECKER

OR

A PET LLAMA?

SAIL IN A BOAT

OR

RIDE IN A HANG GLIDER?

WOULD YOU RATHER...

WEAR YOUR GRANDMA'S CLOTHES

OR

DRESS LIKE A BABY IN DIAPERS?

BE ABLE TO GLOW IN THE DARK

OR

SEE IN THE DARK?

WOULD YOU RATHER...

SAVE UP YOUR MONEY

OR

SPEND IT ALL NOW?

HOLD A SNAKE FOR
AN HOUR

OR

A MOUSE FOR AN HOUR?

WOULD YOU RATHER...

BE A NINJA

OR

A PIRATE?

SWIM WITH DOLPHINS

OR

RIDE A CAMEL?

WOULD YOU RATHER...

LIVE IN AN ACTION MOVIE

OR

LIVE IN A DISNEY CARTOON?

HAVE A GARDEN FULL OF ROSES

OR

SUNFLOWERS?

WOULD YOU RATHER...

SLEEP NEXT TO A SKUNK

OR

A COW?

LIVE ON THE TOP FLOOR OF A VERY TALL BUILDING

OR

ON A RANCH WITH ANIMALS?

WOULD YOU RATHER...

LEARN TO BREAK DANCE

OR

DO THE MOONWALK?

GO SWIMMING IN A RIVER OF COFFEE

OR

DIVE INTO A POOL OF MELTED ICE CREAM?

WOULD YOU RATHER...

EAT CHOCOLATE CAKE

OR

PIZZA?

EAT A DEAD COCKROACH

OR

GET STUNG BY A BEE?

WOULD YOU RATHER...

PLAY IN A BAND

OR

BE ON STAGE IN
A MUSICAL?

PLAY VIDEO GAMES

OR

PLAY OUTSIDE?

WOULD YOU RATHER...

RIDE IN A FERRARI

OR

ON A HORSE?

LOSE YOUR HEARING
FOR A YEAR

OR

LOSE YOUR EYESIGHT FOR
A MONTH?

WOULD YOU RATHER...

EAT PEPPER FLAVORED DONUTS

OR

SALT FLAVORED CANDY?

KISS A BABY CHICKEN

OR

HUG A TURKEY?

WOULD YOU RATHER...

LIVE IN A HOUSE MADE OF CHOCOLATE

OR

A HOUSE MADE OF PIZZA?

SAIL ON A YACHT

OR

GO HANG GLIDING?

WOULD YOU RATHER...

GIVE YOUR OWN SECRET
HANDSHAKE

OR

A HIGH FIVE?

BE ABLE TO TURN YOURSELF
INTO A GIANT BUTTERFLY

OR

A BALD EAGLE?

WOULD YOU RATHER...

EAT FROM DAD'S PLATE

 OR

GRANDMA'S PLATE?

HAVE A BATH IN
BAKED BEANS

 OR

ICE CREAM?

WOULD YOU RATHER...

TRY TO FLY A KITE IN
A HURRICANE

OR

A SNOWSTORM?

RIDE A SKATEBOARD

OR

A SCOOTER?

WOULD YOU RATHER...

HAVE THE WINGS OF
A BAT

OR

THE TEETH OF A BAT?

PLAY INSIDE

OR

PLAY OUTSIDE?

WOULD YOU RATHER...

SEE AN AMAZING FIREWORKS DISPLAY

OR

SPEND THE NIGHT AT THE CIRCUS?

BE REALLY GOOD AT DRAWING

OR

AN AMAZING SINGER?

WOULD YOU RATHER...

HAVE TO READ FOR 6 HOURS A DAY

OR

NOT KNOW HOW TO READ AT ALL?

RIDE ON AN OSTRICH

OR

A PONY?

WOULD YOU RATHER...

HAVE NO FINGERS

OR

NO EARS?

TRAVEL TO ANOTHER GALAXY

OR

TRAVEL THROUGH TIME?

WOULD YOU RATHER...

HAVE TO PEE EVERY HOUR

OR

POOP EVERY HOUR?

NEVER SPEAK AGAIN

OR

NEVER READ AGAIN?

WOULD YOU RATHER...

GO TO THE BEACH

OR

THE SNOW?

PLAY THE DRUMS

OR

THE GUITAR?

WOULD YOU RATHER...

BE 4 FEET TALL

OR

8 FEET TALL?

BE ABLE TO TALK
TO DOGS

OR

CATS?

WOULD YOU RATHER...

HAVE ONE EXTRA ARM

OR

ONE EXTRA LEG?

BE INVISIBLE

OR

SUPER STRONG?

WOULD YOU RATHER...

BE A GIANT MOUSE

OR

A VERY SMALL GIRAFFE?

HAVE A TAIL THAT WAGS WHEN YOU ARE HAPPY

OR

A NOSE THAT GROWS WHEN YOU TELL A LIE?

WOULD YOU RATHER...

PLAY BY YOURSELF

OR

PLAY WITH YOUR FRIENDS?

HAVE A BOWLING ALLEY IN YOUR HOUSE

OR

A FREE MOVIE THEATRE NEXT TO YOUR HOUSE?

WOULD YOU RATHER...

DRINK SOUR MILK

OR

EAT A ROTTEN APPLE?

WAKE UP WITH A KITTEN
IN YOUR BED

OR

A PUPPY IN YOUR BED?

WOULD YOU RATHER...

HAVE NO HAIR

OR

HAVE BRIGHT GREEN HAIR?

JUMP IN A BOUNCY CASTLE WITH A TURTLE

OR

A SNAKE?

WOULD YOU RATHER...

LIVE IN A TREEHOUSE

OR

IN A TENT?

HAVE SIX LEGS

OR

SIX ARMS?

WOULD YOU RATHER...

HOLD A LIZARD

OR

KISS A SNAIL?

HAVE A TINY HEAD

OR

A FURRY FACE?

WOULD YOU RATHER...

BE ABLE TO FLY

OR

TALK TO ANIMALS?

RIDE ON A HORSE

OR

A UNICORN?

WOULD YOU RATHER...

TAKE A SELFIE WITH A MONKEY

OR

A LLAMA?

OWN A HORSE

OR

HAVE A PET SKUNK?

WOULD YOU RATHER...

ONLY EAT JELLY

OR

ONLY EAT PEANUT BUTTER?

ALWAYS SMELL LIKE ORANGES

OR

ALWAYS SMELL LIKE POPCORN?

WOULD YOU RATHER...

HAVE A GENIE'S LAMP

OR

A TALKING DOG?

READ BOOKS

OR

PLAY VIDEO GAMES?

WOULD YOU RATHER...

PLAY BASEBALL

OR

SOCCER?

GO TO SCHOOL BY RIDING
A GIANT KITTEN

OR

A CAMEL?

WOULD YOU RATHER...

SEE A BEE THE SIZE OF AN ELEPHANT

OR

AN ELEPHANT THE SIZE OF A BEE?

WATCH CARTOONS

OR

AN ACTION MOVIE?

WOULD YOU RATHER...

SING REALLY LOUDLY

OR

DO A CRAZY DANCE?

RUN FOR 2 MILES

OR

CRAWL FOR 1 MILE?

WOULD YOU RATHER...

GO ON A VACATION WITH YOUR FAMILY

OR

STAY HOME WITH YOUR FRIENDS?

BE BOILING HOT ALL DAY

OR

FREEZING COLD ALL NIGHT?

WOULD YOU RATHER?

EWW! YUCK! GROSS!

This way to crazy, ridiculous
and downright hilarious
'Would You Rathers?!'

WARNING!
These are Eww! These are Yuck! These
are Gross! And they are really funny!
Laughter awaits!

RatherFunnyPress.com

WOULD YOU RATHER...

WEAR DIRTY UNDERWEAR

OR

WET UNDERWEAR?

HAVE CHEWING GUM STUCK IN YOUR HAIR

OR

STUCK UP YOUR NOSE?

WOULD YOU RATHER...

FART NEXT TO YOUR GRANDMA

OR

YOUR GRANDMA FART NEXT TO YOU?

SNIFF A DOG'S BREATH

OR

A CAT'S BREATH?

WOULD YOU RATHER...

EAT A BOWL OF
WRIGGLING WORMS

OR

A BOWL OF DEAD
COCKROACHES?

EAT A ROTTEN CARROT

OR

LICK A TOILET BOWL?

WOULD YOU RATHER...

EAT A RAW EGG

OR

LICK A MOUSE?

EAT A ROTTEN HAMBURGER

OR

LICK A SMELLY CHILD'S SHOE?

WOULD YOU RATHER...

POO YOUR PANTS

OR

PEE YOUR PANTS?

LICK YOUR BEST
FRIEND'S EYEBALL

OR

EAT A ROTTEN
TOMATO?

WOULD YOU RATHER...

EAT 3 WORMS

OR

LICK A BIRD POO
STAINED BENCH?

HAVE YOUR FARTS SOUND
LIKE A CAR HORN

OR

A CAT PURRING?

WOULD YOU RATHER...

HAVE YOUR FARTS SMELL
LIKE APPLE PIE

OR

KFC?

HAVE A CAT FART
ON YOU

OR

A DOG FART ON YOU?

WOULD YOU RATHER...

HAVE A JOB PICKING
UP DOG POOP

OR

HORSE POOP?

WEAR A USED BABY DIAPER
ON YOUR HEAD AT SCHOOL

OR

GO TO SCHOOL WEARING
A DIAPER?

WOULD YOU RATHER...

TOUCH YOUR FLOATING
POOP

OR

TOUCH A DOG POOP IN
THE PARK?

PICK YOUR FRIEND'S
NOSE

OR

CUT THEIR TOENAILS?

WOULD YOU RATHER...

KISS A WILD RAT

OR

EAT AN EARWIG?

FIND A COCKROACH HIDING IN YOUR CHEESEBURGER

OR

IN YOUR UNDERWEAR?

THANKS A BUNCH!

For reading our book!
We hope you have enjoyed these
'WOULD YOU RATHER?'
scenarios as much as we did as we were
putting this book together.
If you could possibly leave a review of our
book we would really appreciate it. 😊

To see all our latest books or leave a review
just go to
RatherFunnyPress.com
Once again, thanks so much for reading!

P.S. If you enjoyed the bonus chapter,
EWW! YUCK! GROSS!
you can always check out our brand new book,

WOULD YOU RATHER?
EWW! YUCK! GROSS!
for hundreds of brand new, crazy and ridiculous
scenarios that are sure to get the kids rolling on the
floor with laughter!
Just go to:
RatherFunnyPress.com
Thanks again! 😊

YOUR FREE SURPRISE GIFT!

To grab your free copy of this brand new, hilarious Joke Book, just go to:

go.RatherFunnyPress.com

Enjoy!

RatherFunnyPress.com

Made in the USA
Middletown, DE
25 July 2023

35701548R00064